Leopard and Me

Patricia A. Shaw

Illustrated by Nick Roberts

Published by New Generation Publishing in 2020

First Edition

Paperback ISBN: 978-1-80031-670-6
Hardback ISBN: 978-1-80031-669-0
Ebook ISBN: 978-1-80031-668-3

www.newgeneration-publishing.com

New Generation Publishing

For Rachel
and
Uncle Stewart

Leopard and Me

"Where is Leopard?" Abbie looked round and then went to where she was playing.

"Here he is!" she shouted, as she skipped back to her seat.

She sighed with relief and carried him over towards Zita and Uncle Jack. She cuddled and stroked his soft golden furry coat and familiar black, spotted markings.

Leopard went everywhere with Abbie, ever since Uncle Jack bought him as a beany toy in a shop and gave him to her. That was eight months ago, for her 3rd birthday. He was really her closest companion and she felt lost without him.

"You must look after him better than that Abbie," said Zita, biting into her juicy apple.

"Yes," said Uncle Jack. He was wearing his stripy jacket, his straw Panama hat and red trousers. "He came all the way from New York."

It was warm and sunny at Pooh Sticks, the Winnie-the-Pooh trail in Ashdown Forest. Leopard sat next to Abbie enjoying the picnic with her older brother, Andy, and their friends Lizzie, Zita and Uncle Jack. The ground was very dry and hard with tufts of yellow grass.

All their favourite food was laid out. There were chicken drumsticks, pasta, rice salad, tomatoes, cheese, green salad, bread, sausages and lots of different drinks: orange juice, apple juice, lemonade, Coca-Cola and a half-frozen 2-litre bottle of orange squash. When they all had enough to eat and drink, Uncle Jack led them up to the North Pole, where they posed for the annual photo. This was a large rock in the colder part of the Forest. As the children ran down the grassy hill, Mum asked Abbie, "Where is Leopard?"

"Dad is holding him," she said.

"I don't think so," said Mum.

"I remember; he is sitting on the grass in the bag. I will go and get him," said Abbie.

They searched the long grass in hope. "He must be here!"

They climbed back up the slope but when they were at the top, Leopard was not there.

"Abbie sweetheart, I think someone has taken him," said Zita sadly. "Come Abbie, he's not here." Mum went over to stop her from searching between the bushes. Abbie turned and hugged her, sobbing. They walked back to where the others were, Abbie looking behind to see if he would magically appear but he was not there.

When it was time to go home, Abbie sat at the back of the car and looked at the empty rucksack. She begged, "Can we go back and look one more time?"

"Sorry Abbie, we can't. It will be dark soon. Uncle Jack might be able to get another leopard."

"But you can't replace him. Leopard is my closest friend. Oh Mum!" she wailed.

"Don't worry, we will get you a different friend. Leopard has probably gone to a nice safe home. He will be well looked after."

Poor Abbie. She turned towards the window in the car and cried herself to sleep.

One day there was a surprise. "Abbie, there is a letter for you," said Dad.

"Let me see it," answered Abbie eagerly.

"Well you have to be very careful when you open it as it is an airmail letter," he smiled. "It is very easy to tear it open quickly and ruin it."

Abbie opened the thin blue envelope carefully.

She gasped.

"It's from Leopard!" With wide eyes she showed Andy.

"It can't be."

"It is! Mummy, look." She couldn't believe it herself but there it was: Leopard dressed in a scarf, mittens and a hat.

"Where did he go?" Abbie asked confused.

"Let's all sit down and I will read it," said Dad.

"No, I want to!" Abbie took the delicate letter and started to read it.

"'Dear Abbie, sorry ... what does that word say?"

"We will read together." Abbie sighed and then sat on Dad's lap. Andy sat next to him on the sofa. Then they all began.

" 'Dear Abbie,

Sorry I wandered off but I got bored waiting. I went back but you had gone. This very kind girl picked me up and took me home.

Then after a few days, we went on an aeroplane to Germany. It was so exciting.

We have been doing so much siteseeing together. How is school? How are all our friends?

I do miss you. I will tell you all about it when I come home.

Well I must dash, my apple strudel is getting cold.

I will write again soon.

T.T.F.N

Leopard." '

Abbie was beaming!

"How did he get there?" asked Andy.

"We must tell Uncle Jack," decided Abbie.

Before bedtime, the usual story was read and then Abbie read the letter again – with Dad's help.

The next day on the way to school, she was so excited. "We might hear from Leopard again."

"No Abbie. He will write again but not for a while."

"Oh, but he said soon," she said sadly.

"Yes soon."

But the months passed. Christmas came and went, with no letter from Leopard.

"It's snowing! Come Andy!" said Abbie. It was a cold January morning. As she stared out of the window, she said unhappily, "Leopard would love this snow. I do wish he was here to play with me." Andy put his arm round her shoulders and said,

"Come on, Abbie never mind, we will have so much fun!" They ran downstairs eagerly, quickly got breakfast, put their wellies on, scarves and gloves, then went outside into the garden.

At lunchtime they heard the letterbox go. "Oh, it must be the post. Can you get it please someone?" asked Mum.

"I will." Abbie went upstairs.

"Mum!" she said suddenly. "Leopard has written again!" She bounded down the stairs and ran into the kitchen, with another airmail letter. She read her name and quickly opened it. "Where has he been?" Abbie asked, handing Mum the letter.

"America," Mum replied.

Then she began to read:

" 'My dear Abbie,

I hope you are well. I am in New York.' "

"Wow," said Andy

" 'It is so cold and there is so much snow. There is no school today. The snow is so deep, white and fluffy! The snow is as soft as cotton wool. We have been playing snowball fights, building a snowman and drinking steaming hot chocolate with marshmallows on top.

It is fun playing in the snow but I can't wait for some warmer weather. Take care, I will write soon.

T.T.F.N

Leopard.' "

"Mum, can I write to him? I am so sorry he missed playing in the snow with us." Abbie looked up to her Mum pleadingly, with beautiful brown, tearful eyes.

"I am not sure you can as there is no address. But you can write it and Uncle Jack will pass it on," said Mum.

"When Dad comes home, will he help me?"

"Of course he will dear."

"Yeah! I can't wait."

As soon as Dad arrived, she got pencil and paper, settled down at the table and Abbie began to tell him what to write.

Dear Leopard,

How are you?

It is snowing today and I made a snowman with Andy. I am really sorry you could not be with us to play in the snow.

I am going to give this letter to my Uncle Jack to post to you.

I miss you so very much.

T.T.F.N.

Abbie

She was so happy.

After that, Leopard would write once every month. He travelled to so many places. Then after a while he stopped writing. Many months passed and no word was sent from Leopard. Every day, Abbie checked the post, "Anything for me?"

"No Abbie, not this time."

Sometimes Abbie would check herself, to see if she could spot her name under all the post. Then she would look really sad and shrug her shoulders, when nothing was sent to her, or she could not see his lovely handwriting.

Summer was here again. July was as hot as ever. It was a Saturday morning so Mum could have a little extra sleep. Andy and Abbie played quietly downstairs, while Dad read the paper. The letterbox went and Abbie's little feet ran to the door.

"Mummy, Mummy, Leopard has sent a letter."

Mum's lie-in was at an end. Abbie bounded up the stairs and pushed the door open.

"Where has he been?" Abbie asked excitedly.

Mum rubbed her eyes and read.

"Leopard has been to Cuba!" She grabbed the letter and ran downstairs excitedly." Andy, Dad, I've got a letter from Leopard. He is now in Cuba. Mum, come and hear what he is doing."

They sat down on the sofa and, read all that Leopard had been up to. "Mum, what is it like in Cuba?"

"It is very warm, soft sandy beaches and lots of sunshine."

"One day, I am going to Cuba," she smiled.

The day arrived for Pooh Sticks. They woke early, but it was drizzling.

"Our picnic spot will be a bit damp," said Dad, looking out of the window. Soon they packed their picnic lunch and got into the car.

Just then the post-woman came running towards them, just as Dad was getting into the car. "I have something for a Miss Abbie," said the post-woman.

"That's me, it is from my friend, Leopard." She put her hand out of the window and took the letter. "Thank you Miss post lady."

"You're are very welcome."

"Mum, read it please."

"Let us get into the car and I will read it on the way."

"Where has he been?" she asked.

"He has been to Australia!"

When they arrived at Pooh Corner, their friends spread the blanket and they sat down to eat. The dark clouds melted away, the sun appeared and with it blue skies. Then Abbie said, "I have got lots of postcards and letters from Leopard. He has been to Germany, Denmark, New York, Cuba and ... Australia."

"That is the other side of the world," said Andy.

Abbie showed everyone the latest postcard.

As everyone settled down to eat the lovely food, Uncle Jack asked,

"Abbie, would you like a bit of my rice salad?"

"No thank you."

"Oh go on, you would love it. Let me give you a little bit."

Abbie didn't want to be unkind to Uncle Jack but she made a face. She really didn't want it. Uncle Jack went round to Abbie and placed a spoonful on her plate. As he did this, Abbie looked at her Mum with pleading eyes and whispered,

"Mum, I don't like it."

"Never mind, I will help you," Mum said.

Uncle Jack then went back to his seat, smiling.

Abbie tried to push the rice into the furthest part of her plate.

Mum watched her and then saw something next to her. She quickly looked away and pretended she was speedily eating. All the adults saw it. As Abbie pushed the rice away, she looked down next to her and froze.

She looked up at Mum, confused.

"What's wrong Abbie?" asked Mum.

Abbie looked again down beside her and then up at her Mum. Then she whispered, "Mummy, Leopard is back!"

"Where?"

"Here he is!" Abbie held Leopard up aloft and then held her beloved, furry friend close to her. There was a great big smile on her dimpled cheeks.

"He's back! He's come back!" she cried excitedly.

Everyone laughed and laughed.

"Where did he come from?" asked Lizzie.

"Yeah, where did he come from?" echoed Andy. "How did he get here?" Abbie didn't care where he came from, she just continued to hold him close to her. They all looked at Uncle Jack. He just sat down, cunching on his celery stick and beamed.

When it was time to go home, Abbie sat Leopard in the corner of her car seat. As they were on the way home Abbie said, "Mum, Leopard looks a bit different. He's a bit thin and dusty."

"So would you be. He is a year older," Mum said.

"Abbie," exclaimed Andy, "He has been all over the world!"

"Yes he has, and now you have him back," said Dad. Abbie held him in her arms.

"This has been the best day ever. Leopard, I missed you so much. You are not going anywhere without me anymore."

They said goodbye to their friends and drove home. Abbie held Leopard tightly and soon fell asleep.

Leopard smiled. He was back home where he belonged. Leopard never went travelling again - on his own.

Also by Patricia A. Shaw

Patricia A. Shaw

The
Lost Gloves

Illustrated by Nick Roberts